Barbie™

The Story of
Sleeping Beauty

"Can we read this story tonight, Barbie?" asks Stacie.

"Sleeping Beauty is one of my favorite stories!" exclaims Barbie.

Once upon a time, a beautiful baby girl was born to a king and queen.

The king and queen named their daughter Beauty.

They invited everyone in the kingdom to a special party.

Beauty had three fairy godmothers
who brought her magical gifts.

"You will be the most beautiful in all the land."

"You will have the loveliest voice in all the land."

But before the third fairy godmother gave
Beauty her gift, something terrible happened.

The wicked fairy was angry because she had
not been invited to the party.

"I have a gift for the baby, too!" cried the wicked fairy.

"When your daughter grows up, she will prick her finger on a spindle and fall dead!"

"I can't undo the evil spell, but I can make it better," said the third fairy godmother. "Princess Beauty will not die if she pricks her finger on a spindle. Instead, she and everyone in the kingdom will fall into a deep sleep."

Connect the dots to see what a spindle looks like.

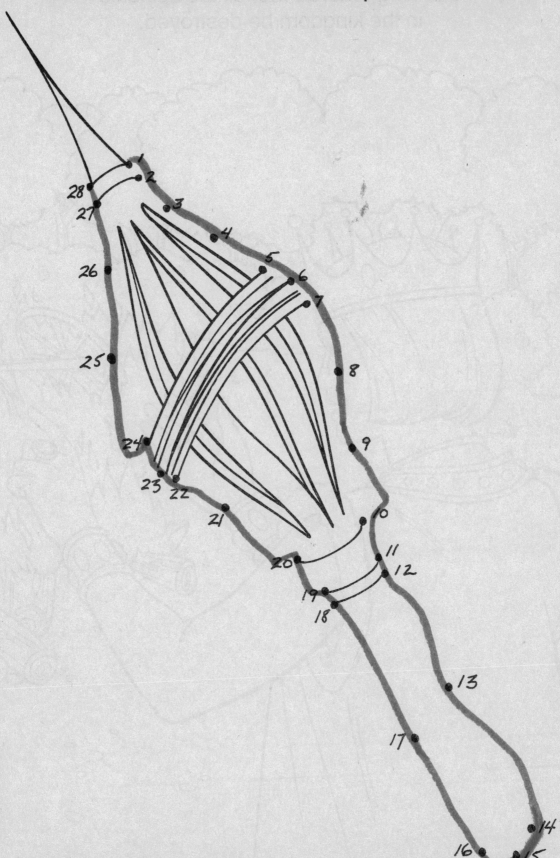

The king ordered that all the spindles
in the kingdom be destroyed.

Can you find the words below in this puzzle?
Look up, down, forward, and backward.

BEAUTY **SPINDLE** **QUEEN** **WICKED FAIRY**
CASTLE **KING** **SPELL**

```
S  P  E  L  L  A  R  E  W  D  L
A  B  S  G  R  I  N  C  E  T  R
W  I  C  K  E  D  F  A  I  R  Y
B  L  A  U  W  R  O  H  T  O  L
E  Y  S  H  O  Q  U  E  E  N  I
A  L  T  S  T  E  Y  G  X  E  P
U  A  L  O  L  K  I  N  G  S  P
T  H  E  T  U  R  V  L  E  E  P
Y  E  S  S  P  I  N  D  L  E  H
```

Just as the first fairy godmother had said, Beauty grew up to become the most beautiful young woman in all the land.

© 1998 Mattel, Inc.

Beauty did not know about the spell
the wicked fairy had put on her.

How many words can you make from the letters in the word
BEAUTY?

_____

_____

_____

_____

_____

_____

_____

_____

_____

_____

Possible answers: be, tea, buy, yet, tab, bat, tub, at, beat, eat, ate, but

Beauty loved to explore the castle.

One day, she found a door she had never seen before.

There were steps leading to a tower room.

© 1998 Mattel, Inc.

"Hello! My name is Beauty. Who are you?"

The old woman was really the wicked fairy!
She was busy at her spindle.

The old woman invited Beauty to touch the spindle . . .

... and the princess pricked her finger!

"I feel so tired," said Beauty. "I must lie down."

"Good night, Sleeping Beauty!" cackled the wicked fairy.

"And good riddance to you and the kingdom!"

The king, the queen, and the whole kingdom
also fell into a deep sleep!

As everyone slept, time passed.
Thick branches with thorns grew around the castle.

Soon, only the tip of the tower could be seen.

Inside the tower, Sleeping Beauty remained in a deep sleep.

One day, a prince heard the story of
Sleeping Beauty. He set out to find her.

A path of roses led the Prince to Sleeping Beauty's castle.

Choose the correct path to help the Prince find his way to Sleeping Beauty's castle.

FINISH

START

Answer:

The Prince made his way to the castle.

"The princess must be in the tower!" cried the Prince.

The Prince found Sleeping Beauty at the top of the stairs.

Perhaps a kiss would break the spell.

The spell was broken! Sleeping Beauty
awoke from her slumber.

Word List:

KISS   **SPINDLE**   **DEEP SLEEP**
PRINCE   **ROSES**   **TOWER**

Across

1. What did Beauty prick her finger on?

4. What woke up Sleeping Beauty?

5. Beauty fell into a _____ _____.

Down

2. Who woke Sleeping Beauty?

3. Where was the old woman?

6. What lined the path to the tower?

Answer:

As everyone awoke, the castle once again came to life.

The king and queen had a splendid party to celebrate.
Sleeping Beauty and the Prince danced together all night.

Circle the picture that is different in each row.

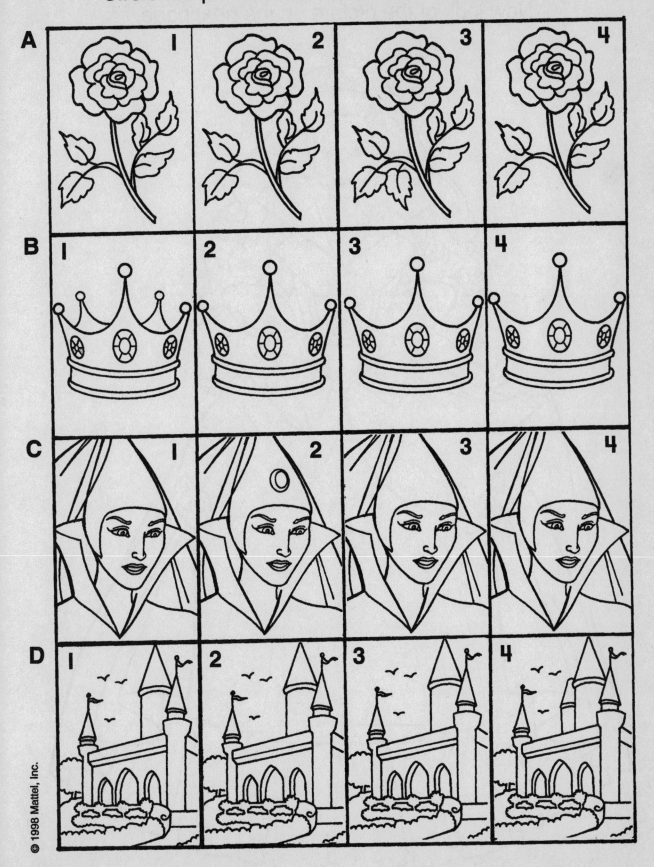

Answers: A=3; B=1; C=2; D=4

Look at the picture on this page.
Now look at the picture on the next page.

How many differences can you find?

Answers: tiara, necklace, lace on dress, sparkles, lacing on bodice, bow on waist

The Prince asked Sleeping Beauty to marry him.

Sleeping Beauty was very happy and truly
the most beautiful in all the land.

The Prince and Sleeping Beauty
were married and lived happily ever after.

"Now it is time for you to be a sleeping beauty, too!"